Nothing at All

by DENYS CAZET

Orchard Books   New York

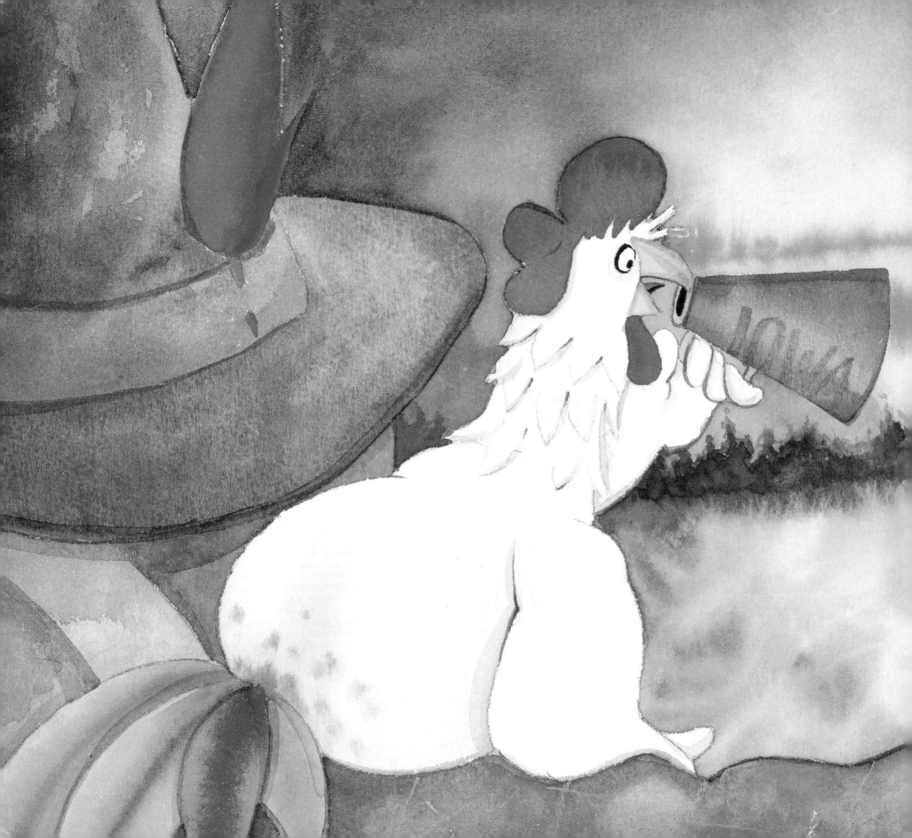

"Cock-a-doodle-dooooo! Good morning to you!"

The horse woke up with a grin and a sneeze,
pranced about, raced about, racing the breeze.
"Neighhhh!" said the horse. *"I slept like a filly!"*

The cow woke up with a kink in her back,
indigestion, a headache, an udder attack.
"Moooooooo!" said the cow. *"I'm in a terrible mood."*

Out in the meadow,
The breeze strolled by,
And the scarecrow listened.

Can you guess what he said?

Nothing at all!

The sheep woke shyly, oh, so neatly,
slipped off their pajamas, so discreetly.
"**Baaaaaaa!**" said the sheep. "**Please . . . no peeking!**"

The piggies stretched and threw mud on their faces,
then spread it around in all the best places.
"*Oink, oink!*" said the piggies.
"*Always bathe before eating.*"

Out in the meadow,
The breeze strolled by,
And the scarecrow listened.

Can you guess what he said?

Nothing at all!

Ten little chicks scratched and dug,
then politely shared a banana slug.
"Cluck, cluck!" said Mama.
"See how delicious good manners can be!"

The dog, dog-tired, heard the chickens cheep, sighed, rolled over, and went back to sleep. "**Woof!**" said the dog. "**Too early!**"

Out in the meadow,
The breeze strolled by,
And the scarecrow listened.

Can you guess what he said?

Nothing at all!

In the meadow, the cat was stalking, watching, waiting, softly talking.

"Meooowwww!" said the cat. *"I see my breakfast!"*

The mouse grew nervous when she saw the cat,
then ran off quickly, no time for a chat.
"Squeak!" cried the mouse. **"Where will I hide?"**

Out in the meadow,
The breeze strolled by,
And the scarecrow listened.

Can you guess what he said?

He pursed his lips
And jiggled his hips
And performed three backward
Double back flips.

He beat out a beat
Like a rock 'n' roll rocker
And rapped out a rap
Like a rap happy squawker.

A heel kicking hoofer,
A boot stomping stomper,
A tap dancing dancer,
A berserking berserker.

He whirled and twirled
Around and around
Until the mouse flew out
With a little mouse sound.

The scarecrow collapsed,
Twisted and scattered.
He lost his great head
And the stuffing that mattered.

"Scarecrow, you scared us.
We thought you were dead!"
But the scarecrow wasn't. . . .

Can you guess what he said?

For my grandson
JAKE,
aka Jonathan Scott

Orchard Books, 95 Madison Avenue, New York, NY 10016

Manufactured in the United States of America. Printed by Barton Press, Inc. Bound by Horowitz/Rae.
Book design by Mina Greenstein
The text of this book is set in 24 point ITC Symbol Medium. The illustrations are watercolor and
colored pencil reproduced in full color.   10 9 8 7 6 5 4 3 2 1

Library of Congress Cataloging-in-Publication Data
Cazet, Denys. Nothing at all / by Denys Cazet.   p.   cm.   "A Richard Jackson book" — Half t.p.
Summary: As the farm slowly comes to life, each animal stirs and speaks in his own distinctive voice,
but the scarecrow says nothing until he discovers a mouse in his pants.
ISBN 0-531-06822-6.   ISBN 0-531-08672-0 (lib. bdg.)
[1. Domestic animals — Fiction.   2. Animal sounds — Fiction.   3 Scarecrows — Fiction.
4. Morning — Fiction.]   I. Title.   PZ7.C2985No 1994   [E] — dc20   93-25204